KAY THOMPSON'S ELOISE

Eloise Has a Lesson

STORY BY **Margaret McNamara**

ILLUSTRATED BY **Kathryn Mitter**

Aladdin Paperbacks

NEW YORK · LONDON · TORONTO · SYDNEY

🫖

ALADDIN PAPERBACKS
An imprint of Simon & Schuster Children's Publishing Division
1230 Avenue of the Americas
New York, NY 10020
Copyright © 2005 by the Estate of Kay Thompson
All rights reserved, including the right of reproduction
in whole or in part in any form.
"Eloise" and related marks are trademarks of the Estate of Kay Thompson.
ALADDIN PAPERBACKS, READY-TO-READ, and colophon are
registered trademarks of Simon & Schuster, Inc.
Art direction and design by Cheshire Studio
The text of this book was set in Century Old Style.
Manufactured in the United States of America
First Aladdin Paperbacks edition January 2005
14 16 18 20 19 17 15 13
Library of Congress Cataloging-in-Publication Data
McNamara, Margaret.
Eloise has a lesson / written by Margaret McNamara ;
illustrated by Kathryn Mitter.— 1st ed.
p. cm. — (Ready-to-read) (Kay Thompson's Eloise)
Summary: Eloise would rather tease her tutor,
Philip, than let him teach her math.
ISBN 978-0-689-87367-6 (pbk.)
1113 LAK
[1. Teachers—Fiction. 2. Teasing—Fiction. 3. Arithmetic—Fiction.]
I. Mitter, Kathy, ill. II. Title. III. Series. IV. Series: Kay Thompson's Eloise.
PZ7.M47879343En 2005
[E]—dc22
2004009343

I am Eloise.
I am six.

I am a city child.

I live in a hotel
on the tippy-top floor.

This is Philip.

He is my tutor.
He is no fun.

Here is what I do not like:
doing math
for one half hour
in the morning.

Here is what I like:
teasing Philip.

Philip says, "Hello, Eloise."

I say, "Hello, Eloise."

Philip says, "Math time."

I say, "Bath time?"

Philip says, "Eloise, please."

I say, "Eloise, please."

Philip says,
"What is five plus six?"

I say, "You do not know?"

"Nanny!" says Philip.
"Make Eloise behave."
"Eloise, behave," says Nanny.

Chalk makes a very good straw.

"What is five plus six?"
says Philip.

"Five plus six is the same as
six plus five," I say.

Philip says, "Oh, Eloise."

I say, "Oh, Eloise."

Nanny says,
"Math time is nearly over.

"Time to finish up, up, up."

Philip says, "Eloise."

I say, "Philip."

Philip says, "Think."

I say, "I am thinking."

Philip says,
"What is five plus six?"

"It is eleven," I say.
"And the lesson is over."

Ooooooooo,
I absolutely love math.